Giants of the Ocean

HALF and HALF

GREAT STORY & COOL FACTS

Introduction

Welcome to Half and Half books, a great combination of story and facts! You might want to read this book on your own. However, the section with real facts is a little more difficult to read than the story. You might find it helpful to read the facts section with your parent, or someone else, who can help you with the more difficult words. Your parent may also be able to answer any questions you have about the facts—or at least help you find more information!

Giants of the Ocean

English Edition Copyright © 2008 by Treasure Bay, Inc.
English Edition translated by Wendy Helfenbaum and edited by Sindy McKay

Original edition Copyright © Éditions Nathan (Paris, France), 1999
Original Edition: Les géants des mers

Rescued by a Dolphin by Jean-Lou Craipeau
Illustrated by Miles Hyman

Non-fiction text by Brigitte Dutrieux
Illustrated by Éric Alibert, Franck Bouttevin, Pierre de Hugo, Olivier Nadel,
Jean-François Poissenot, Bernard Rocamora; Vignettes: Colonel Moutarde.
Puzzle Game: Dominique Billout
True or False quiz and anecdotes: Bruno Ollier

Photo Credits :
M. L. Simion/Rapho; coll. Jonas/Kharbine-Tapabor;
S. Westmorland/Fotogram-Stone Images;
S. Baldwin/copyright 1995 WB Prod. LTD/Monarchy Enterprises

Special thanks to Jim Harvey, Professor of Marine Science
at Moss Landing Marine Laboratories, for his review and comments
on the non-fiction material for this book.

Published by Treasure Bay, Inc.
P.O. Box 119, Novato, CA 94948 USA

PRINTED IN SINGAPORE

Library of Congress Catalog Card Number: 2008920814

ISBN-13: 978-1-60115-212-1

Visit us online at:
www.HalfAndHalfBooks.com

PR 11-14

Giants of the Ocean

Table of Contents

Story: Rescued by a Dolphin

Facts: Sharks, Dolphins, and More!

Rescued by a Dolphin

A Sailor's Story

I knew the sailor was quite old, but when I was a child, I thought he was immortal. It seemed that he had been sitting in that rocking chair forever, staring out towards the ocean, as if waiting for someone to return. My friends and I would often gather on the porch of his beach shack, hoping to hear a story of his adventures at sea.

There was one story we loved more than all the others combined, and we would ask for it everyday. Most days, the old sailor just shook his head and chose another tale.

Sometimes, however, he would murmur, "This is a good day to remember the girl from Cuba and the great gray dolphin."

We would draw closer as he cleared his throat and began:

Storm at Sea

"I was young then," he said. "I was just twelve years old and already working as a deckhand on a small fishing boat. There were only three of us on the *Neptune:* Captain Vara, Pedro and me.

One day, a violent storm rose up and surprised us with its fury. Our boat was tossed and thrown by the powerful wind. I was filled with terror as I listened to its timbers tremble and squeak, threatening to splinter.

Captain Vara was amused by my fear and inexperience. "Careful, boy," he wickedly teased, "These gusts can suck up a lightweight sailor like you and hurl him into the sea!" Then, he laughed cruelly, as I clung to the railing, my stomach churning like the ocean around me.

At last, the sky cleared and the waves calmed. Captain Vara started the engine and turned toward home. But, after several hiccups, the engine died and refused to start again.

Captain Vara was not laughing now.

Without the power of the engine, our boat was no more than a helpless cork bobbing in the water. The shore, too distant for anyone to detect our distress, seemed lost to me.

As Pedro struggled to repair the engine, he both cursed and pleaded to Neptune, the god of the deep sea, whose name was proudly displayed on the helm of our small boat.

"Don't just stand there!" growled Captain Vara as he hung a pair of binoculars around my neck. "Search the ocean for a rescue ship!"

Exhilarated by the huge responsibility thrust upon me, I forgot about my seasickness and put the binoculars to my eyes. I stared out across the water, wide-eyed.

The Shark

At first, I couldn't believe what I saw: behind the walls of water, a mast was dancing. Once the swell calmed, I saw that it was a raft.

In the middle of the raft, gripping the mast, was a young girl about my age. Her red dress was soaking wet and in her hand she held a doll dressed all in white. I waved my arms, but she did not see me. Her attention was focused on the water in front of her. What was she looking at? I followed her gaze down to the water's surface and saw what she was seeing.

It was a shark's fin.

I shouted to the Captain and he grabbed the binoculars to look.

"It's a young girl from Cuba, no doubt," he informed me. "Probably embarked on that raft to escape the poverty of her country."

"We have to help her!" I pleaded.

The Captain shook his head. "Without our engine, we can do nothing." Then, he gave me back the binoculars and walked away.

Quickly, I searched the sea for the shark's fin. I soon found it advancing slowly toward the raft, as if working up its courage.

Suddenly, it disappeared beneath the surface. A moment later it resurfaced, mouth gaping open to reveal its huge teeth! In a shower of foam, its jaw slammed shut onto a section of the raft, tearing off part of the floor. The girl from Cuba covered her eyes and screamed in terror, dropping her

doll into the water! Its white dress filled with air, helping the little doll stay afloat.

The shark ripped through the water, attacking the floating debris from the broken raft. The young girl reached her hand out desperately towards her doll. But the doll was just out of reach . . .

The menacing fin once again cut through the waves and swam towards the raft, preparing for battle.

At that moment, a happy band of five young dolphins with white stomachs and dark backs, seemed to appear from out of nowhere. They began to leap and dive around the fearsome beast. Suddenly, and without warning, the powerful body of the shark was jolted! It was as if a giant torpedo had arisen from the depths of the ocean to strike. The beast was thrown into the air, then slapped back down with a huge splash. It was stunned for a moment—then took flight.

"He's gone!" I yelled. "The shark is gone!"

Captain Vara rushed over to look. I pointed toward the raft where the young dolphins were making a big fuss over a large gray dolphin, which now swam among them.

"He saved her! That dolphin saved the girl!" I shouted.

The Captain stared. "It's him," he whispered in awe. "The great gray dolphin I almost captured."

He turned and shouted back to Pedro. "Pedro! Quick! Come look!"

Pedro was beside him in an instant. He whistled in appreciation when he saw the great gray animal. "That is him, Captain. Over 8 feet long and probably 300 pounds!"

"I would have set a record, if he hadn't gotten away," Vara muttered.

"You should have seen it, Pedro," I exclaimed. "That great gray dolphin smacked the shark on its side and tossed it into the air!"

Pedro nodded. "Dolphins do not like sharks. Sometimes, they even attack them."

"Do they bite them?" I asked.

Captain Vara grunted scornfully, "Hah. You don't know anything, do you, boy? Dolphins strike their enemy in the stomach and burst their liver!"

My cheeks burned with embarrassment, so I turned away from my shipmates and back to the girl. The five young dolphins were gone now, but the great gray was circling the raft. It seemed that he was guarding her and I could see that she was now calm and secure.

By the magic of this special friend, the sea no longer appeared hostile to me, either. The wind had calmed, the swells had diminished, and the water sparkled under the clear sky.

The great gray put his head on the edge of the raft and the young shipwrecked girl knelt to hug him. I watched her caress his lustrous skin and speak to her rescuer for a long time. Through my binoculars I could see tears running down her rounded cheeks.

What was she saying to him? Was she telling him the story of her old life? About her parents? Her country? The terrors she had endured when the sea swallowed the people that were accompanying her?

She gestured towards the ocean and I knew she was searching for her doll.

The great gray nodded his head and rubbed his muzzle against her fragile shoulder. Then he let himself slip into the water, which swallowed him without a single splash.

As I waited to see if the dolphin would return, I heard Pedro and Captain Vara speaking behind me.

"It's too bad that one got away from you, Captain," remarked Pedro.

"Yes. It's too bad . . ." said Vara, curiously quiet.

The Great Gray Dolphin

"There he is!" I shouted with a smile.

The great gray dolphin had returned. In his mouth, delicately held between his small pointed teeth, was the girl's doll. When he placed it onto the raft, the young girl from Cuba clasped her hands in joy. The dolphin seemed to nod his head in understanding of her thanks. Then he slipped again into the water and began somersaulting around the raft, swimming upright, hitting the water with his head and his fins, whipping through the waves, straddling them. I thought he was playing the clown to reassure his young friend. But he was doing much more than that.

As he jumped and played, the great gray was actually moving the raft towards us. In no time, she was close enough for us to hoist her onboard.

I could tell that she was desperately thirsty and hungry. I gave her food and water, and soon she seemed to be feeling much better. She giggled when I played with her doll, pretending to be a mother rocking a baby. The great gray dolphin also seemed to be laughing, as he chattered and clicked and nodded his head.

But while we played, Captain Vara was scheming . . .

From the corner of my eye, I saw him lift the sharp harpoon we sometimes used on our expeditions to land big fish. I turned and shouted, "What are you doing?"

"He got away once—he won't get away again." the Captain ominously replied.

Fleeing the Harpoon

He raised the harpoon higher, ready to pierce the great gray with its metal point. The young girl from Cuba understood the danger. Clutching her doll, she threw herself into the water without hesitation. She grabbed the dolphin's fin and shouted for him to flee.

The great gray reared back, avoiding the point of the harpoon. Like a mighty steamship, he moved away from us, cutting through the waves with the young girl astride his back. As the great gray dolphin and the girl from Cuba headed towards the shore, I had the impression of the sea opening to honor a legendary animal.

Land At Last

I turned to the Captain, tears of anger in my eyes. "I will never go out to sea with you again," I swore.

The shore suddenly seemed even more distant. I was certain I would never see land again . . .

Pedro continued to work on the engine, but it was no use. We kept watch the rest of the day, trying to draw the attention of the few ships we saw from afar. With no success, the Captain and Pedro finally drifted off to sleep. For a long time, the fear of this sea that breathed beneath me like the back of a live monster kept me awake. But finally, I too fell asleep. It was still dark when I awoke again, feeling now as if I was sailing among the stars. I sat up, aching and sticky with seawater, and realized that the Neptune really was gliding swiftly and quietly through the water.

It was the great gray dolphin steering us along.

Before long, we were crossing the canal of a small fishing port and the boat stopped moving. I watched as the dolphin gracefully disappeared in the wake of the moonlight. I wondered about the young girl from Cuba, who was no longer on its back. I felt certain he had dropped her off safely some-where on the island.

For years, I thought that one day I would see her, perhaps walking down the beach or stepping off a boat. But I never saw her or the dolphin again. That is why, each day that I have left, I sit in this rocking chair and watch the sea, hoping . . ."

The old sailor's voice would often trail off at the end of his story. He would sigh and look past us, over the rolling waves, with a sad smile on his face.

A Final Goodbye

Today, the village led the old sailor to his final resting place. I thought he was immortal, but he was not.

After the funeral services, I noticed an elderly woman. A Cuban woman. Once the crowd had left, she approached and placed a doll on the old sailor's casket.

Now, the spirit of the great gray dolphin will watch over him forever . . .

Living
in the Water

Fish survive differently in the water than marine mammals. Each has adapted to this element in its own way.

Breathing

Fish breathe using their gills, which extract oxygen from the water. Marine mammals, on the other hand, cannot breathe in the water. They must resurface to breathe air with their lungs.

Moving around

Much of the weight of animals in the ocean is supported by the water. Thus, the skeletons of marine animals do not need to support their body's weight like land animals do. It is for this reason that the skeleton is less developed in most marine animals. Also, rather than limbs, they have fins to propel their bodies through the water.

■ Finding their way around

Toothed whales and dolphins can find obstacles and prey by emitting sound waves that bounce back to them when they hit an object: this is called echolocation. Echolocation is very similar to the sonar* used in submarines.

*Sonar
A detection and underwater communication device that uses sound waves.

Electric detection
Sharks can sense the tiny electric charges in their prey.

■ An original way to feed itself
Certain marine animals, and also many invertebrates*, feed themselves by filtering the water. As they filter the water, they catch tiny animals, as well as plant and animal debris.

*Invertebrates
These animals do not have a spinal column.

17

Sharks—Fish with a Bad Reputation

Three types of shark teeth

White shark

Tiger shark

Blue shark

Sharks grow more teeth to replace the ones they lose. Over several years, a shark can lose several thousand teeth.

Their sense of smell is remarkable: they can smell blood in the water several miles away. They also have an amazing sensor, called the ampullae of Lorenzini, situated under the skin of their head and muzzle. This sensor can help sharks find their prey by detecting the tiny electric charges which are created in the bodies of other animals.

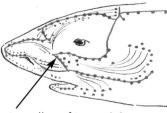

Ampullae of Lorenzini

The largest sharks usually travel alone, but certain species, such as the hammerhead shark, sometimes move in groups of over one hundred.

When a shark bites . . .

Its muzzle lifts up.

Its jaws are independently projected to the front.

■ Sharks are Endangered

The oil from sharks' livers is used in the cosmetics industry. Their cartilage serves in the manufacturing of medications to treat burns. In parts of Asia, shark fins are considered a delicacy for soups. Many species of sharks are hunted and are endangered, but no species is currently protected.

Sharks don't have scales on their skin like most fish do, but instead they have small tooth-like structures called dermal denticles.

Sharks do not have bones. Their skeleton is made up only of cartilage.

■ Eggs or babies?

Certain shark species, such as rock salmon, lay eggs. Others, such as angel and hammerhead sharks, give birth to babies. With the nurse shark, the eggs actually hatch inside the female's body!

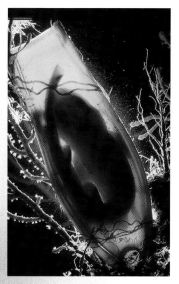

Shark egg stuck to seaweed

Some Shark Species

■ Are sharks dangerous?

Only about twenty species are dangerous to man. There are usually less than thirty reported cases of fatal attacks each year. Nets or devices creating an electronic field are used to protect swimmers and divers. Anti-shark suits are being studied.

Numbering around three hundred and fifty species, we know less about sharks than almost any other fish in the ocean.

Meaning for the symbols you will find in the notes for various animals:

DANGEROUS TO HUMANS

ENDANGERED SPECIES

VERY LARGE!

FAMOUS ANIMAL

Great white shark

Size:	up to 23 feet
Food:	fish, seals and sea lions
Living area:	coasts

Distinguishing features:

This is the shark with the "teeth of the sea"

Distribution: all oceans

Carpet shark

Size:	up to 11 feet
Food:	mollusks and shellfish
Living area:	rocky or coral reefs and sandy sea beds

Distinguishing features:

Enormous flat head in the shape of a disk. Its skin color merges with the bottom of the sea.

Distribution: Australia, New Guinea and Japan

Whale shark

Size: can reach almost 40 feet
Food: plankton
Living area: at the surface
Distinguishing features:

The largest fish in the world. Often travels in groups

Distribution: Pacific, Atlantic and Indian Oceans

Saw shark

Size: 3 to 3.5 feet
Food: fish, squids, and crustaceans
Living area: deep muddy or sandy sea beds
Distinguishing features:

long, saw-like snout, which is edged with teeth

Distribution: Atlantic, Pacific, and Indian Oceans

Basking shark

Size: about 30 feet
Food: plankton and shellfish
Living area: coast and high seas
Distinguishing features:

gills have tiny teeth meant for filtering water

Distribution: Pacific and Atlantic Oceans, Mediterranean Sea

Great hammerhead shark

Size: about 18 feet
Food: fish, squid and shellfish
Living area: coasts
Distinguishing features:

Muzzle in the shape of a hammer. Nostrils and eyes are located at each end of the enlarged muzzle

Distribution: tropical waters and hot climates

Tiger shark

Size: about 18 feet
Food: anything that can be eaten!
Living area: mainly on the coasts
Distinguishing features:

Marbled skin, like that of a tiger. Dangerous to man

Distribution: tropical waters and hot climates

Angel shark

Size: about 3 feet
Food: fish, mollusks and shellfish
Living area: on the sea bed, up to 1200 feet deep
Distinguishing features:

resembles rays, often half-buried in the marine sea beds during the day

Distribution: temperate waters and tropical seas

21

Rays and Torpedoes

These fish spend much of their lives half-buried in the sand or the mud.

Stingray

■ Do they look like bats?
The skin and teeth of rays are similar to a shark. But rays can be distinguished from sharks by their flat shape and their highly developed pectoral fins, which look like wings. Some rays have a tail shaped like a whip.

■ Venom
Certain rays, such as the stingray, possess a tail that contains a poisonous sting. They can be very dangerous.

Thornback ray

Stinger

Manta ray

Size: 22 feet
Food: Plankton
Distinguishing features:

has horns on its head; lives in couples or small groups; often leaps out of the water; has one baby at a time

Distribution: tropical seas

■ Eggs or babies?

Thornback rays hatch their eggs. The eggs are protected by rectangular-shaped capsules that are often found empty on beaches. The English call them "mermaid's wallets"! Other rays give birth to their young, such as torpedo rays or manta rays

Thornback ray

Size: 3 feet
Food: fish, shellfish and mollusks
Distinguishing features:

back covered with large thorns

Distribution: Atlantic Ocean and Mediterranean Sea

Electric lobes

■ Electric Shock

Electric rays, including torpedoes, are equipped with electric organs that release shocks that can paralyze their prey. Electric rays have been used in medical research in hopes of finding treatments for diseases of the nervous system.

Marbled torpedo

Size: 3 feet
Food: fish, shellfish and mollusks
Distinguishing features:

bad swimmer; gives electric shocks of 45 to 80 volts, which are painful but not dangerous

Distribution: Atlantic Ocean and Mediterranean Sea

A Whale's Life

Perfectly adapted to aquatic life, these mammals even give birth under water.

A baleen whale's blow

A sperm whale's blow

The height and look of the blow allows us to identify the different species of whales.

■ A powerful blow

When it emerges, a whale exhales the moist air from his lungs through its blowholes (baleen whales have double blowholes, while toothed whales have just one). This "blow", which looks like a white cloud, can reach heights between 15 to 25 feet, in the case of the sperm whale. Then the animal inhales the air through its blowhole in preparation for its next dive.

■ On the menu: meat or shrimp?

Toothed whales capture living prey such as octopus, squid and fish. Whales with baleen filter the water to catch krill, tiny shrimp-like animals that live abundantly in polar waters. In spring, large numbers of whales travel thousands of miles to gorge on krill for the summer. In the fall, the whales return to warmer waters and eat practically nothing until the following summer.

Different kinds of acrobatics
Most whales do spectacular jumps
from the water. Scientists think they
do this to communicate amongst
themselves, to play or to attract
a partner.

Giving birth under water
The whale's gestation* lasts
many months and the baby,
usually just one, comes
into the world with its
tail out first. A Blue
whale baby measures 20 feet
and weighs two tons! The
mother whale nurses her
baby underwater for a
few months.

Gestation
The period during
which the baby lives
inside its mother's
womb

25

Beluga Whale

Size: 15 feet
Food: fish
Living area: water between ice floes

Distinguishing features:
nicknamed "canary of the sea" due to the many high pitched sounds it makes; completely white

Distribution: Glacial Arctic waters

Cetaceans are mammals. They all have tail fins that are oriented horizontally, and nostrils called blowholes.

Cetaceans

Who are the cetaceans?

Within the group of cetaceans are two types of whales: baleen whales and toothed whales. (By the way, dolphins are whales!)

Right Whale

Size: around 48 to 50 ft.
Food: copepods
Living area: cold or temperate waters

Distinguishing features:
its name comes from the fact that it was considered the "right" whale to hunt; very large lower "lip" covers its baleen.

Distribution: Arctic, Atlantic and Northern Pacific Oceans

Endangered

Blue Whale

Size: from 75 to 100 ft.
Food: krill
Living area: all oceans

Distinguishing features:
the largest animal in the world; numerous folds along the lower jaw to its pectoral fins.

Endangered

Sperm Whale

Size: 49 to 59 feet
Food: squid
Living area: very deep waters
Distinguishing features:

lives in groups of many males and females. *Moby Dick,* the hero of Herman Melville's book, is a white sperm whale

Distribution: all the oceans

Endangered

Narwhal

Size: 13 to 15 feet
Food: fish, squid and krill
Living area: ice-belts
Distinguishing features:

nicknamed 'unicorn of the sea' for its single twisted horn

Distribution: glacial Arctic waters

–Some with Teeth, Some with Baleen

Baleen:
Long horn-like plates suspended along the upper jaw, which filter and trap plankton.

Humpback Whale

Size: 40 to 50 feet
Food: krill and fish
Living area: all oceans
Distinguishing features:

a hump in front of the dorsal fin; the males have a complex song

Distribution: Northern Pacific and Atlantic Oceans

Endangered

27

The Whale Hunt

For many hundreds of years and in oceans around the world, man has been hunting whales.

The Basques and the Right Whale

In the tenth century, the Basques became masters in the art of fishing for the Right Whale. It was the ideal whale: it rarely measured more than 50 feet, and it was harmless and slow. And it continued to float even after it was dead, which enabled the fishermen to drag it right into shore.

Harpoon vs. the Whale

The Norwegians were probably the first whalers. In the Middle Ages, whale-hunting was particularly dangerous: armed with hand-held harpoons and sailing on small, fragile boats, the fishermen risked their lives over and over again as they faced the giants of the ocean.

Endangered Whales

By the early twentieth century, whale hunting began to severely diminish the numbers of whales in the world. In 1946, The International Whaling Commission (IWC) was created to help manage and protect the whale population. Members of the IWC agreed to a halt in 1986 on almost all whale hunting. Since then, most countries have banned or severely restricted whale hunting and the numbers of some whale species have been increasing. However, the United States Fish and Wildlife Service still lists 8 whale species as Endangered: Blue Whales, Bowhead Whales, Finback Whales, Gray Whales, Humpback Whales, Right Whales, Sei Whales, and Sperm Whales.

Invented in 1868, the harpoon-launching canon revolutionized hunting. It enabled hunters to attack larger and faster whales: one load of powder from the harpoon could explode in the animal.

A dive into the great blue sea

All these animals lounge about in their liquid environment. But how many are fish, and how many are mammals? While you're counting fish and mammals, see if you can find the nine errors that have slipped into this picture.

Answers on page 41

Dolphins
and Porpoises

Porpoise

Dolphin

Playful and acrobatic dolphins, which live in groups, are easier to observe than their more shy cousins, the porpoises.

Not to be confused

Porpoises are sometimes confused with dolphins. Compared to dolphins, the muzzles of porpoises are shorter and their teeth are shaped like spatulas. Porpoises are among the smallest of the cetaceans. They are also more shy and fearful of people than dolphins are. This may be one of the reasons that they are not known or studied as much as dolphins are.

Inside a group of dolphins, there's an understanding: dolphins help sick individuals to swim up to the surface to breathe, and protect them from predators.

■ Jumps and stunts

Dolphins often display acrobatics as they jump from the water. The jump probably fulfills many functions: attracting a partner, exchanging information with other individuals, or simply playing!

■ Fish for dinner

To catch fish, you have to be fast. Often, a group of dolphins will work together to catch a meal. As soon as the dolphins have spotted a school of fish, they gather and force them to the surface. Then the dolphins jump out of the water, while whistling, and hit the water with their tails. The frightened fish near the surface seem to be easier prey for the dolphins.

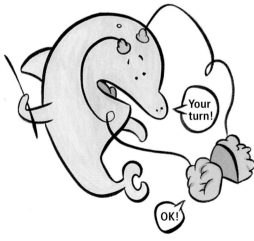

Your turn!

OK!

■ A brain that never sleeps

For a dolphin, breathing is not a reflex but rather a voluntary act, a command from its brain. In order not to suffocate while sleeping, it has a particular kind of sleep: the right half of its brain sleeps for twenty minutes, while the left side stays awake in order to control its breathing. Then, the process is reversed.

A Little Help, Please!

Dolphin Lifeguards

Greek and Roman legends often feature sailors and dolphins. In one legend, it was a dolphin that rescued Ulysses' son from drowning.

In 1993, in England, a group of dolphins saved three men by pushing a small boat stuck in a storm towards shelter. Many stories like this have been told.

■ Caught in a trap

Each year, many dolphins die when they accidentally get caught in fishing nets. People and organizations are trying to get owners of fishing boats to change their nets, so they are less dangerous to dolphins.

Some Dolphin Species

Pilot whale

Size: 12 to 20 feet
Food: fish and squid
Living area: cold, temperate and tropical waters

Distinguishing features:
dorsal fin tilted towards the rear

Distribution: all the oceans

Bottlenose dolphin

Size: 6 to 12 feet
Food: fish and squid
Living area: cold, temperate and tropical waters

Distinguishing features:
lives in small groups

Distribution: all the oceans

Common dolphin

Size: 5 to 7 feet
Food: fish and squid
Living area: hot, temperate and tropical waters

Distinguishing features:
signature 'V' on its flanks; very acrobatic; emits a number of high-pitched squeals; lives in groups

Distribution: all the oceans

Orca (Killer Whale)

Size: 18 to 32 feet
Food: fish and seals
Living area: great deep, estuaries and interior seas

Distinguishing features:
the biggest dolphin; usually lives in groups; doesn't attack man, in spite of its name of 'killer whale'; acrobatic and curious

Distribution: mostly coastal areas, deep estuaries and interior seas

Harbor Porpoise

Size: 4 to 6 feet
Food: fish
Living area: mainly cold coastal waters

Distinguishing features:
it also travels through rivers over long distances

Distribution: Northern Hemisphere

The Orca

The orca is also known as a killer whale, but is really a type of dolphin

■ Sedentary or nomadic?

There are two types of killer whales. Sedentary ones live in a given region in groups of five to twenty-five individuals and eat mostly fish. Nomads move around over large areas in groups of one to seven individuals. They eat seals, fish and even whales!

■ The giant among dolphins

With its black and white suit and its enormous dorsal fin, the killer whale is easy to identify. It is not uncommon to see these animals leaping out of the water and turning around to land on their flanks. Very curious, killer whales are very approachable. Easy to train, they are often captured to be displayed in marine parks.

The male's dorsal fin can grow to almost 5 feet long.

■ When the killer whale breaks the ice

Some killer whales possess a remarkable technique to capture seals, which are resting on ice-floes. Once the seal is spotted, a killer whale dives and with one powerful burst, resurfaces to break the ice and dislodge the surprised seal. It is capable of breaking off a block of ice more than a meter thick. If the block is too thick, the killer whale pushes down one side to tilt it and make the seal fall into the waiting mouth of another killer whale!

Incredible, but True!

Cetacean Record

Cetaceans have, in their ranks, champion divers. Sperm whales can dive deeper than three thousand feet and can resurface very quickly. Bottlenose whales are able to spend two hours underwater before resurfacing to take a well-deserved gulp of fresh air.

Cannibalism Among Sharks

In the bodies of certain female sharks, a drama is unfolding. Before they are born, the biggest and most developed baby sharks eat their brothers or sisters who are smaller than them.

Answers to the puzzle on pages 30-31

There are forty-four fish and nineteen mammals, including the men. Here are the errors you should have found: the dinosaur, the narwhal with two horns (although in very rare cases, narwhals have been known to have two horns), the starfish (or sea star) with seven arms, the dolphin's tail (which is a shark's tail), the mermaid, the hammerhead shark's tail (which is a dolphin's tail), the colors of the killer whale (which are inverted), the frog and the crab's claw.

Seals, Sea Lions and Walruses

These mammals share their time between land and water.

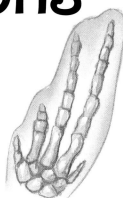

■ Seals

Earless or true seals have strong rear flippers that always point to the back and they do not possess any visible ears. They are more agile in the water than on land. Their fur is short and thick.

The limbs of seals end in webbed flippers. These flippers help them to swim fast and enable them to come onto land, where they reproduce and molt.

Gray seal

Size:	About 6 feet
Food:	fish
Living area:	rocky coasts

Distinguishing features:
spotted, no external ear

Distribution: : Baltic Sea, Northwest and Northeast Atlantic coasts

■ Warning!

Mediterranean monk seals once lived in abundance in the sea, south of Europe. Today, there are only a few hundred left and it is feared that they may soon completely disappear and become extinct.

■ Eared seals

Another group of seals, known as eared seals, have two adjustable rear limbs and visible external ears. They are more agile on land than earless seals. Eared seals include fur seals and sea lions. Walruses are a related, but different type of marine mammal.

Walrus

Size: about 11 feet
Food: mussels, clams, shells, sea urchins, fish...
Living area: coasts near icebergs
Distinguishing features:
males and females have two long tusks that curve downwards

Distribution: Arctic coasts

Fur seals

Size: 4 to 6 feet
Food: fish
Distinguishing features:
visible ears and a thick, downy, wooly coat

Distribution: Atlantic and South Pacific oceans

The vibrissae, hairs located on the muzzle of seals and walruses, → help them to sense the movements of their prey.

Sea Lion

Size: 4 to 8 feet
Food: fish and squid
Living area: coasts
Distinguishing features:
visible ears, smooth hairs applied against the skin; roars (similar to a lion's roar) or barks

Distribution: Pacific Oceans

Hunting for Seals

All these marine mammals have been killed by the millions for their thick layer of fat. Baby seals and sea lions have also been hunted for their fur, and walruses for their ivory tusks. Hunting has been restricted, and many of these animals are now more protected.

Unusual Marine Mammals

◼ Mermaids?

Long ago, some sailors might have thought they were seeing a mermaid, when they saw a manatee or a dugong. This is one theory about how the myth of mermaids got started.

◼ Front flippers

They use their front flippers to "walk" on the sea bottom, to scratch or bring food up to their mouths. Female manatees also use their front flippers to hold their babies in their arms.

◼ Endangered

Both manatees and dugongs live an entirely aquatic life and both are, unfortunately, very endangered.

Manatee

Size:	8 to 14 feet
Food:	marine grasses and seaweed
Living area:	fresh or salt water

Distinguishing features:
usually solitary

Distribution: near the coasts of North and South America

Dugong

Growk!

Size: about 8 feet
Food: marine grasses and seaweed
Living area: hot and shallow marine waters

Distinguishing features: often live in groups; the males possess two elongated incisors protruding from their mouths

Distribution: Indian Ocean, Coasts of Africa, Persian Gulf and India, Indonesia and Australia

Dugongs have a split rear fin; manatees have a rear fin that is not split.

◼ Sounds of an unknown origin

Manatees and dugongs moan and growl. But since they do not possess vocal chords, scientists cannot figure out how these sounds are emitted. The sounds probably serve as communication between individuals.

◼ An extinct species

The Steller's Sea Cow was related to manatees and dugongs. It could attain 24 feet in length and lived near the mouth of rivers in the Bering Sea. After its discovery in 1741, it was hunted to extinction in only 27 years.

Reptiles of the Sea

Certain species of turtles, as well as crocodiles and snakes, live in the sea.

■ Saltwater Crocodile

The natural habitat of the saltwater crocodile is estuaries and marshes along Asian coasts. It is the largest type of crocodile (up to 20 feet) and also one of the most aggressive towards man. This mostly nocturnal animal feeds on fish. Once hunted for its skin, it is now protected in many areas.

■ Sea Turtles

Many species of turtles live in the ocean. They all possess flat front flippers to help them swim and rear flippers they use as rudders. Contrary to land turtles, they cannot pull either their heads or their flippers under their shell. These animals are known for their long migrations, but they always return to the same beaches to hatch their eggs.

Hawksbill Turtle

Size: up to 3 feet
Food: sponges, vegetation, jellyfish, urchins
Living area: coral reefs
Distinguishing features:
Tortoise-shell combs and eyeglass frames used to be made out of the shell of this turtle; this turtle is critically endangered

Distribution: mostly tropical oceans

◼ Sea Snakes

Many species of sea snakes live along the hot coasts of the Indian and Pacific Oceans. Their flat tail serves as a fin and their nostrils are blocked by a valve when they dive. Some hatch their eggs on sandy beaches, but others do so underwater. The venom from their bite can be fatal.

Leatherback Sea Turtle

Size: up to 6 feet
Food: primarily jellyfish
Living area: hot, temperate and tropical waters

Distinguishing features:
it is the largest living turtle; critically endangered

Distribution: mostly tropical oceans

Green Sea Turtle

Size: up to 4 Feet
Food: mostly algae and sea grass
Living area: calm bays and lagoons

Distinguishing features:
in the past, often used to make turtle soup, this turtle is now endangered

Distribution: mostly tropical oceans

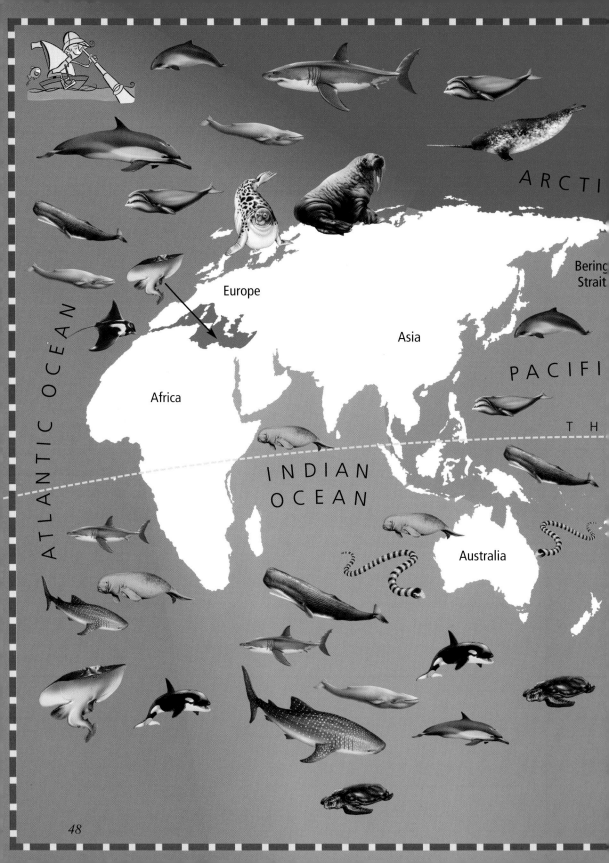

ARCTI

Bering
Strait

Europe

Asia

Africa

PACIFI

T H

ATLANTIC OCEAN

INDIAN
OCEAN

Australia

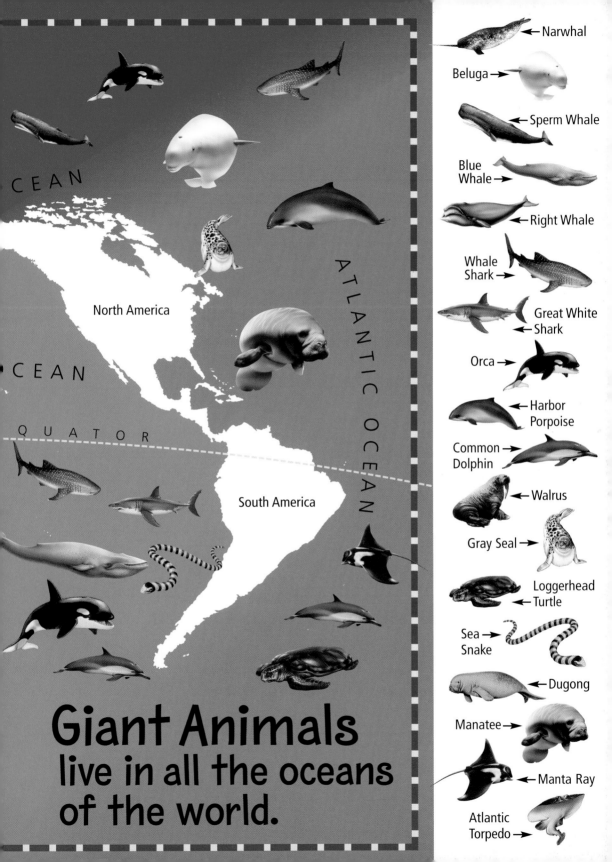

Giant Animals
live in all the oceans of the world.

Narwhal

Beluga

Sperm Whale

Blue Whale

Right Whale

Whale Shark

Great White Shark

Orca

Harbor Porpoise

Common Dolphin

Walrus

Gray Seal

Loggerhead Turtle

Sea Snake

Dugong

Manatee

Manta Ray

Atlantic Torpedo

OCEAN

CEAN

ATLANTIC OCEAN

North America

South America

EQUATOR

Animals of the Abyss

Strange creatures populate the depths of the sea, which represent ninety-three per cent of the ocean's space

The Deep Sea Angler has a long luminous filament used to attract its prey

■ Very difficult living conditions

In the great depths, total darkness reigns, because light cannot penetrate deeper than fifteen hundred feet. The temperature is very low (36 degrees Farenheit). The pressure is enormous, due to the weight of the water. Sources of food are minimal. But in spite of these conditions, many animals live in these regions.

Some food comes from the falling of debris from dead animals and excrement from above. The absence of light stops any vegetation from developing.

Black Smokers

Giant Tube Worm

In a few areas, there are sea vents of hot water at the bottom of the ocean. These areas support giant tube worms and other animal life. Giant tube worms can measure up to 6 feet in length and have a large red plumb that extends out of their tube.

Luminous animals

Many fish, squid and crustaceans of the great deep produce light thanks to some of their cells. They use this light to frighten their enemies or to attract their prey. Other deep sea animals are blind or have very small eyes.

Living Oasis

Scientists have discovered some previously unknown marine animals, some of which are very large. They were living close to hot water vents, called black smokers, more than six thousand feet deep at the bottom of the ocean. Mussels, worms, fish, crabs, shrimp, and octopus have all been found close to these deep sources of hot water.

40 foot long giant squid really exist!

Sperm whales like to eat giant squid. Scars from giant squid suckers have been found on the bodies of many sperm whales.

51

True or False?

Cetaceans
are fish.

False.
They are mammals.

No animals live
in the ocean below
two thousand feet.

Anyone
there?

False.
There is animal life up to about
nineteen thousand feet deep.

Dolphins
do not practice
echolocation.

False.
Whales and dolphins use this
method of sonar to detect their
prey and orient themselves.

The biggest
squid caught
measured
almost 60 feet
in length.

True.

Sharks breathe by using their lungs.

False.
They use gills to take in oxygen.

The saw of the saw shark is wrapped before birth.

True.
It is wrapped in a membrane to avoid injuring the mother before the birth.

A baby blue whale can grow almost 6 inches per day.

True.
Their mother's milk is very nutritious.

The record for the deepest dive by a mammal is held by the sperm whale.

True.
A sperm whale can dive to depths of over 5,000 feet.

The whale's fins are called baleen.

False.
Baleen are long plates attached to the jaw of certain types of whales, used to filter food from the water.